TOBY SPEED

Two Cool Cows

ILLUSTRATED BY

BARRY ROOT

G. P. PUTNAM'S SONS • NEW YORK

Library of Congress Cataloging-in-Publication Data
Speed, Toby. Two cool cows / by Toby Speed; illustrated by Barry Root.   p.   cm.
Summary: Millie and Maude are two cool cows who fly to the moon and back in a night
wearing the Huckabuck children's new black boots. [1. Cows—Fiction. 2. Moon—Fiction.
3. Stories in rhyme.] I. Root, Barry, ill. II. Title. III. Title: 2 cool cows.
PZ8.3.S736Tw   1995   [E]—dc20   93-34258 CIP AC   ISBN 0-399-22647-8
10 9 8 7 6 5 4 3 2 1   First Impression

*Dedicated to my cool friend
and biggest encourager, Steve Fraser*—T.S.

For Victoria Stephenson—B.R.

Over the hills of Hillimadoon and Willimadoon
and Rattamadoon and Hattamadeen,
up the river and down the river
and over the bridge and around the bend
come Millie and Maude,
two cool cows from the Huckabuck Farm.

Two cool cows wearing new black boots
(boots that belong to the Huckabuck kids),
eight black boots on the eight fleet hooves
of the two cool, too cool cows.

How do they go? *Clop! Clop!*
Where do they go? To the mountaintop.
To the mountaintop of Hillimadoon,
the best jumping-off place for the moon,
for cows who are jumping over the moon
in new black button-back boots.

Hey diddle diddle, moon be bright.
Hey diddle diddle, let's jump tonight.
Jump right over the moon!

Ate the grass in the meadow here.
Ate all the grass that was growing here
in Hillimadoon and Willimadoon,
in Rattamadoon and Hattamadeen
and all of the places in between.
Now, where can we go where the grass is green?
To the far, far side of the moon.

Over the rickety pickety fence,
Down through the buggity bog!
Straight through the wickedy thickety woods,
Into the fishety pond!

And right behind come the Huckabuck kids—
Kate, Doug, Daisy, and Spoon.
All the way up to the mountaintop,
four quick kids in their bedroom slippers,
four quick kids with forty cold toes,
all the way up yelling, "Stop! Stop!
Bring back our button-back boots!"

Moon has a meadow, green and wide,
a great green meadow on the other side
for cows on the munch,
cows by the bunch,
ever so many
eating their lunch,
cows in the craters,
cows and their cousins,
cows on vacation,
dozens and dozens.

How do they go? *Clop! Clop!*
What do they do? The bunny hop.
The bunny hop in a meadow of moon.
There's nothing quite like it in Hillimadoon.

And far below cry the Huckabuck kids—
"Come back Millie! Come back Maude!
And bring back our new black
knickknack paddywhack
runamuck Huckabuck
button-back boots!"

One more bite, to fill us up,
of columbine and buttercup.
Buttercup and columbine,
a nibble more, and then it's time.
Time to go—goodbye! Goodbye!

Where do they go? Far, far.
Over the meadow and under the stars.
Over the bluebells and hollyhocks,
back to the kids on the mountaintop,
for it's grass to milk,
and milk to cheese,
and home by seven o'clock.

Hey diddle diddle, moon be bright,
We're running a race with the moon tonight.
Up the river and down the river
and over the bridge and around the bend.
Into the pond! Into the woods!
Into the bog! Over the fence!
Cows, kids, buttons, boots,
back to the Huckabuck Farm.

But moon gets home ahead of the rest.
There's moon in a puddle, and moon in the field,
moon in the hayloft and moon on the shed.
(And it's terribly late for going to bed!)
There's moon on the tractor and there on the barn
of the two cool, too cool cows.

How do they go? *Clop! Clop!*
What do they do? The bunny hop.
Kate plays the fiddle,
little Doug laughs,
and Daisy runs off with Spoon.

And maybe tomorrow we'll do it again—
jump right over the moon!

JE
SPEED

Speed, Toby.

Two cool cows.

$15.95

101542
07/28/1995

DATE			
AUG 23 '95			
AUG 31 '95			